P9-DHI-308

SAM WHO NEVER FORGETS

by EVE RICE

MULBERRY BOOKS • New York

Copyright © 1977 by Eve Rice. All rights reserved. No part of this book may be reproduced without permission from the Publisher,
Greenwillow Books, 1350 Avenue of the Americas, New York, NY 10019. Printed in U.S.A.   First Mulberry Edition, 1987   3 4 5 6 7
Library of Congress Cataloging in Publication Data   Rice, Eve   Sam who never forgets.   [1. Zoo animals—Fiction]   I.   Title.
PZ7.R3622Sam   [E]   76-30370   ISBN 0-688-07335-2

In the park

the zoo clock strikes three.

And every day
at three o'clock
Sam the zookeeper
feeds the animals.

Sam never forgets.

Sam fills his wagon with good things
for the animals to eat.

And then he is on his way.

"Good afternoon, Giraffe," says Sam.
"I have lovely green leaves
 for your dinner."

And that is just what Giraffe likes best.

"Thank you," says Giraffe, and Sam is gone.

"You're welcome" he says.

"Hello, Monkeys!" Sam says
  and hands them yellow bananas.
"Splendid," say the Monkeys.
"Sam never forgets."

Next is Seal. Sam throws him fish.
"Deliciously good!" barks Seal.

And then comes Bear, who loves red berries.
Sam always brings him some.

Sam feeds the hungry Crocodiles

and long-legged Ostrich.

He gives fresh meat to Lion

and oats to quiet Zebra.

Then Sam's wagon is empty.
And off he goes.

But Elephant has not been fed!

He's worried !

And poor Elephant, who is
very hungry, bellows:

"Did you forget?
Oh, Sam!
Did you forget?"

All the animals are very sorry for
hungry Elephant.

But just as a tear starts to fall from Elephant's eye, just as Elephant starts to cry, Sam calls out:

"Forget? I NEVER forget!"

And there Sam is with a wagon full
of golden hay.

"Oh, Elephant! It's just that you're so
<u>awfully</u> big. And you do eat <u>such</u> a lot—

so I've brought you a wagon all your own."

Elephant smiles. "You didn't forget!
And I <u>do</u> so love fresh hay!"

Elephant hugs Sam. "Thank you, Sam!"
And Sam hugs Elephant. "You're welcome"

And just so no one should ever forget,
just so everyone always remembers,

Elephant trumpets: "Hooray for Sam!
Sam who never, ever, never,

Sam who never, never forgets!"